This book belongs to:

Based upon the television series *Bob the Builder*™ created by HIT Entertainment PLC and Keith Chapman, as seen on Nick Jr.® Photos by HOT Animation.

 SIMON SPOTLIGHT
An imprint of Simon and Schuster Children's Publishing Division
1230 Avenue of the Americas, New York, New York 10020

Manufactured in the United States of America
First Edition
10 9 8 7 6 5 4 3 2 1
ISBN 0-689-86180-X
These titles were previously published individually by Simon Spotlight.

Bob's Favorite Fix-it Tales

Simon Spotlight

New York   London   Toronto   Sydney   Singapore

Contents

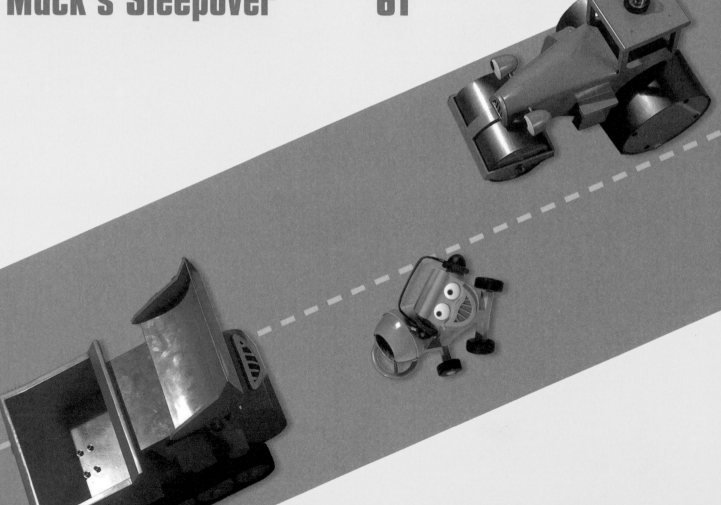

Bob the Builder™

Bob's Birthday

"Listen, everybody!" Wendy exclaimed. "Today is Bob's birthday. Let's pretend it's just an ordinary day and surprise Bob with a party tonight!"

"Won't Bob be disappointed if we don't wish him a happy birthday?" asked Muck.

"We can wish him a happy birthday at the party," Wendy explained. "Now remember, it's a secret. Not a word to Bob!"

Just then Bob came into the yard.

"Hi, Wendy, was there any mail for me?" he asked.

"Were you expecting anything special?"

"Uh . . . no. Nothing special," he said.

He turned to Scoop and Lofty. "We have to go and fix Farmer Pickles's barn."
"Have a good day, Bob," Wendy called.
"I'll try," mumbled Bob as he rolled out of the yard with Scoop and Lofty.
Wendy sighed. "Now I can begin baking Bob's birthday cake!"

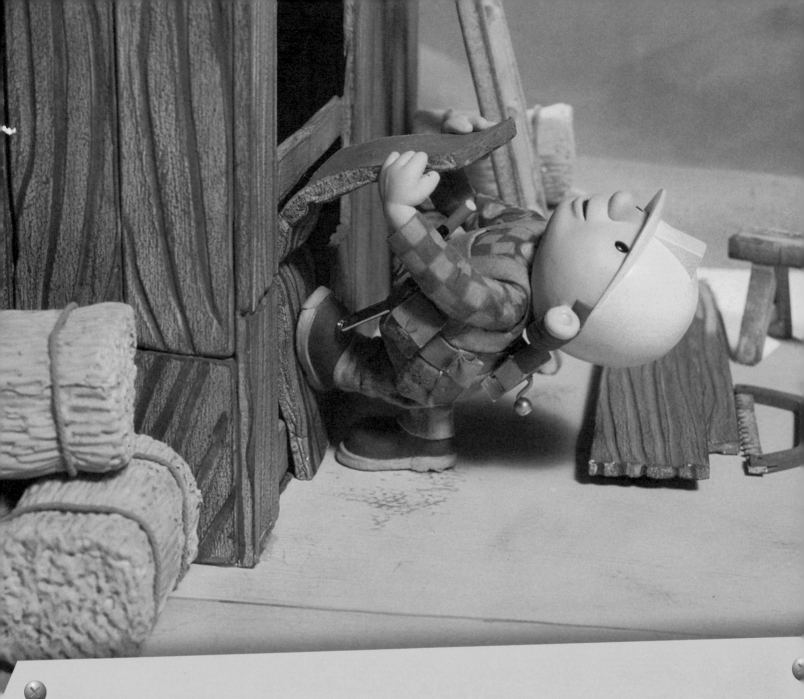

When Bob, Scoop, and Lofty got to Farmer Pickles's barn, Travis and Spud were already there. Bob started to pull the old planking off the wall so he could replace it with new planking.

"Pull harder, Bob!" yelled Spud.

14

"I'm doing my best," grunted Bob. Suddenly the plank came loose
and Bob fell back on his bottom.
Things weren't going that well for Bob on his birthday!

Back at the yard Dizzy and Muck watched Wendy make Bob's birthday cake. "Cake mixing looks easy," said Dizzy. "You just throw everything together and mix it up. Just like making concrete!"

"Hey, why don't we make Bob a concrete cake he can keep forever? **Can we make it?**" asked Muck.

"**Yes, we can!**" exclaimed Dizzy.

Dizzy whipped up a load of her very best concrete. Then she poured it into a tire mold.

Then Roley helped Muck and Dizzy decorate their concrete
cake with some flowers, feathers, and leaves.
"Wow! Cool cake," Roley said.

At Farmer Pickles's barn Bob and Lofty were still working hard. Their work was coming along nicely.

"Travis and Spud, aren't you two supposed to be delivering Farmer Pickles's eggs?" asked Bob.

"You're right!" said Travis, starting up his engine. "Come on, Spud," he called. "I'll drop you off at Bob's house."

At Bob's house, Wendy was done making Bob's birthday cake. "Mmmmmm!" exclaimed Spud as he scooped some icing off the cake and plopped it into his mouth.

"Spud!" Wendy yelled.

"I'm sorry, Wendy," Spud mumbled. "But it looks so good!"

"Do you want to help me put the candles on the cake?" asked Wendy.

"You bet! Spud's on the job!" he laughed.

As Bob nailed the last plank into Farmer Pickles's barn, his cell phone rang. "Maybe this is a birthday phone call," he said hopefully. It was Wendy. "Hi, Bob," she said. "When are you coming home?"

"Actually we've just finished and we are on our way," Bob told her. "Why . . . any special reason?"

"No," Wendy replied. "I've just got a few letters for you to sign. Bye."

"No 'Happy Birthday, Bob'," Bob murmured to himself.

Scoop winked at Lofty. "Come on, Bob. Time to go home!" he said.

25

Back at the yard Wendy, Muck, Dizzy, and Roley had
decorated a table and covered it with cakes and presents.
Bob couldn't believe his eyes when he arrived back at the yard.

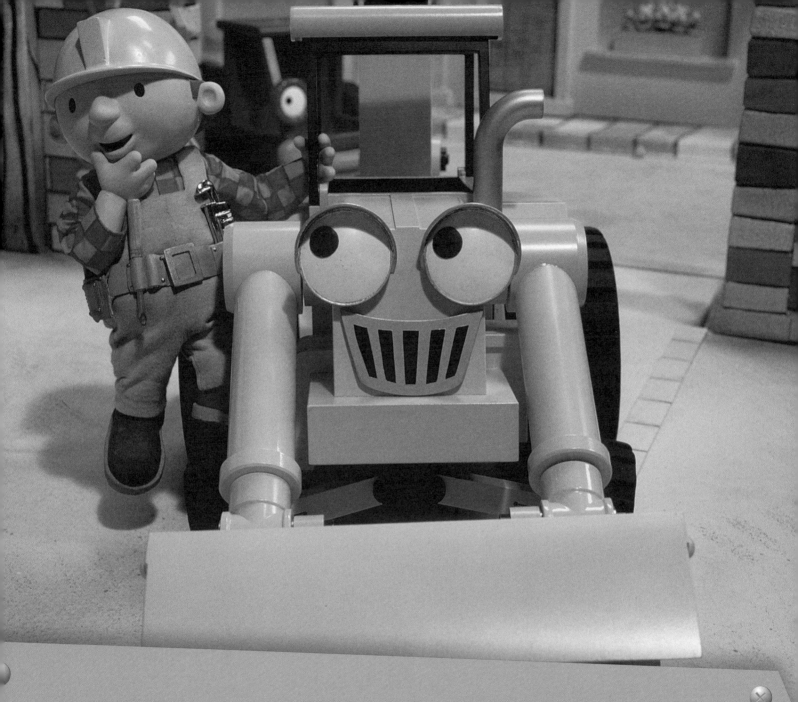

"Surprise!" laughed Wendy.

"I thought you forgot my birthday!" Bob exclaimed.

"Forget your birthday?" Wendy teased. "Never! Look! You've got two cakes—a real cake to eat and a concrete cake you can keep forever!"

27

Everybody burst out singing:

"Bob the Builder, it's his birthday!
Bob the Builder, yes, it is!
It's Bob's birthday, can we sing it?
It's Bob's birthday—yes, we can!"

29

"And don't forget your mail!" Wendy said.

"All these birthday cards for me?" gasped Bob.

"Of course," replied Wendy, "you're the Birthday Builder!"

Everyone cheered, "Hooray!"

"Now can I please have a slice of that yummy-looking
cake?" begged Spud, interrupting.

"Of course you may," said Bob as he cut Spud a huge piece.

Spud stuffed the piece of cake into his mouth and smiled.
"Like I always say: 'I'm on the job, Bob!'"

Bob the Builder
Scoop Saves the Day

It was a wild and stormy night. All across town thunder crashed, lightning flashed, and rain poured down. By morning the storm had stopped, but a lot of damage had been done. Bob was the first person to hear about it.

"Bob! This is urgent," Wendy said, reading a fax aloud. "Roads are blocked and fences are broken. Immediate help is needed!"

"Okay, Wendy," Bob said, handing her his cell phone. "I'm on my way!"

Bob went out into the yard.

"We're needed right away," he said to the vehicles.

"I can dig it," chugged Scoop.

"I can roll it!" rumbled Roley.

Meanwhile Lofty, Muck, and Pilchard went to Farmer Pickles's farm to make sure everything was all right there.

"Look, we need to clean up the pond! C'mon, Lofty!" cried Muck.

While Lofty was piling garbage into Muck's bin, Pilchard
decided to get a closer look at the ducks. She scrambled up the
storm-damaged tree and climbed onto a wobbling branch.

CRACK!

"**Meow!**" cried Pilchard as she dangled over the water.

"Quick, Lofty! Do something! We've got to rescue Pilchard!" exclaimed Muck.

Lofty tried to hook the fallen tree, but he couldn't reach Pilchard.

"Chirp!" whistled Bird, and he flew away.

"Look, Bird's going back to the yard for help," said Muck. "I'll go with him. You stay here and look after Pilchard."

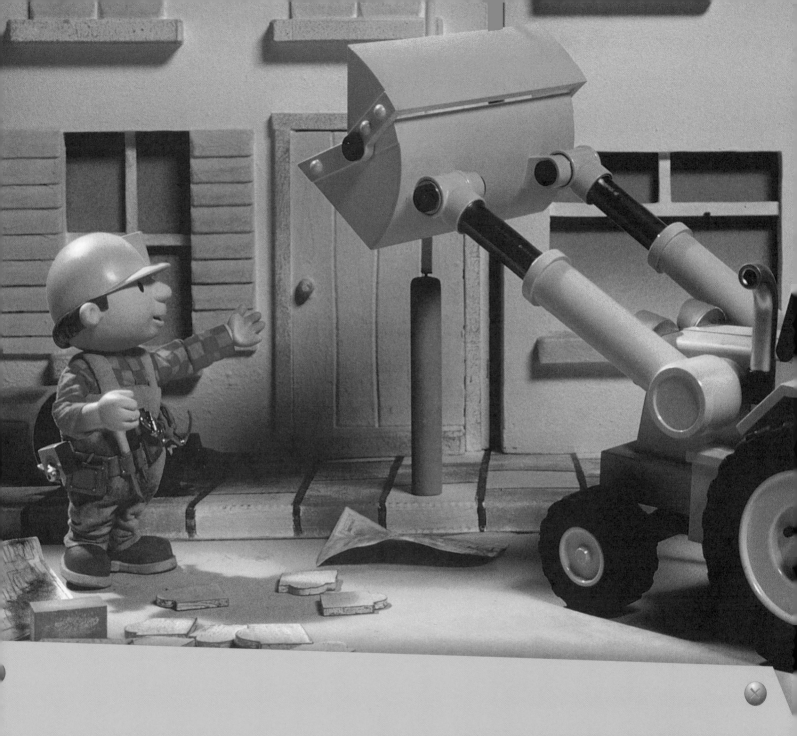

Meanwhile Scoop and Bob were busy clearing a road into town.
"Left a bit . . . that's it. Well done, Scoop," said Bob.

"Help, Wendy!" yelled Muck, rolling into the yard. "Pilchard is stuck in a tree over the pond. And she can't swim!"

"I'll call Bob right away," said Wendy. "Oh, no! Bob didn't take his cell phone!"

"One of us will have to go and get him," squeaked Dizzy.

Across town, Bird found Scoop.

"Bird!" cried Scoop. "What are you doing here?"

"Chirp! Chirp!" Bird explained, hopping up and down. Scoop listened to Bird, wide-eyed. "Bob! Quick!" he called, swinging into reverse. "We've got to go!"

Scoop roared back into the yard.
"There's been an accident," cried Dizzy.
"A tree fell into the pond," Muck said.

"And Pilchard is stuck in the tree," Wendy added.

"Lofty tried to lift the tree . . . but it's too heavy," Muck explained.

"Don't worry," replied Bob. "We're on our way!"
He turned to the vehicles.
"Ready, team?" he called.

"Can we rescue?" shouted Scoop.

"Yes, we can!" shouted everyone.

With their wheels turning as fast as they could go, they all set off for the farm.

Pilchard was very relieved to see Bob and the vehicles riding toward the duck pond.

"Don't worry, Pilchard," said Bob. "We'll have you
out of that tree in no time! But first we have to move
the ducks out of the pond so they don't get hurt."

Scoop picked up the ducks and gently placed them into Dizzy's cement mixer.

"Quack! Quack!" said the ducks.

"Oooh!" Dizzy giggled. "That tickles!"

"Now for Pilchard," said Scoop, and he gently placed his rear scoop under the frightened cat.

"Hop in, Pilchard!" called Bob.

Pilchard leaped off the branch and collapsed into Scoop's bucket.
"There you go," Bob said softly as he picked her up. "You're all
right now."

Everyone was tired when they got back to the yard.

"Good job, team! Now let's get a good night's sleep," Bob
told the vehicles. "We've still got a lot more repair work to do
tomorrow."

When Bob walked into his living room, Pilchard was already asleep in her favorite chair.

"Purr, purr", Pilchard said sleepily.

"Well, I'll be," laughed Bob.

Bob the Builder
Muck's Sleepover

Late one afternoon Wendy, Muck, and Roley were hard at work. They were making a path through Farmer Pickles's field. While Wendy supervised, Muck cleared a trail and Roley smoothed it down.

Farmer Pickles and Travis stopped to say good-bye.

"Goodness," said Wendy. "Is it time to go home already?" Wendy and the machines had been so busy they hadn't noticed the time. "Muck, we'll have to come back and finish the job first thing in the morning."

"Oh, no!" Muck cried. "Does that mean I'll have to wake up early?"

Wendy laughed. "I'm afraid so," she said.

"I know!" Travis piped up. "Why don't you sleep at the farm tonight, Muck?"

Muck had never spent the night away from home before.

"Can I stay, Wendy? Can I pleeeease?" Muck pleaded.

"It's all right with me," said Farmer Pickles. "If it's all right with you."

"Well, okay," said Wendy. "Remember to behave yourself, Muck."

"I will, I will!" Muck promised.

"Hooray!" Travis and Muck cheered.

"Bye, everyone," Wendy said, climbing aboard Roley. "Sleep well!"

Later that evening Muck and Travis settled down in the shed.

"This is exciting!" Muck said. "I've never slept in the country before."

"Is it different from sleeping in town?" asked Travis.

"Oh, yes. In town there are cars going past," Muck told him. "And the streetlights are on all night long."

Travis yawned. "I suppose you find it dark and quiet here," he said sleepily.

Suddenly Muck noticed that it *was* very dark and quiet on Farmer Pickles's farm.

"D-D-Dark and q-q-quiet," Muck said. "Oh, dear."

Nearby, Spud was listening. "It won't be quiet for long," he said, chuckling to himself.

Meanwhile Bob, Scoop, and Lofty were working late.

"What's the job, Bob?" Scoop asked.

"We have to put some safety lights inside this tunnel," Bob said.

"Why do we have to do the job at night?" Lofty asked.

"The tunnel has to be closed off for safety," Bob explained. "The best time to do that is at night when not many people use it."

Inside the tunnel Bob used his drill to attach a long cable to the wall. Then he connected lights to the cable.

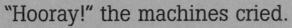
"Now let's make sure it works," Bob said.
He checked the fuse box to make sure everything was safe.
Then he flipped a switch, and bright light filled the tunnel.
"Hooray!" the machines cried.

73

Just then they heard a strange noise. **Hoot! Hoot!**

"That sounds like an owl!" Bob said. "What's it doing in here?"

"Meoooow!" Pilchard dashed off to find the owl.

"Come back, Pilchard!" Bob called. But she was already gone.

"I'd better go after her," Bob said.

Back at Farmer Pickles's farm, Muck was wide-awake. Suddenly a twig snapped. And then another.

"What was that, Travis?" Muck asked.

"ZZZZZZZ," Travis replied, fast asleep.

"Ha, ho-ho!" Spud giggled to himself. He was having fun teasing Muck.

Spud made a spooky noise. "Whooooooooooh!"

"It's just the wind," Muck said nervously.

"Huuack! Huuuuack!" Spud called, making another scary sound.
"Ahhhh!" Muck screamed. "It's a horrible monster!" Quick as
a flash Muck zoomed out of the shed and away from the farm.
"Come back, Muck!" Spud shouted. "I haven't finished scaring you!"

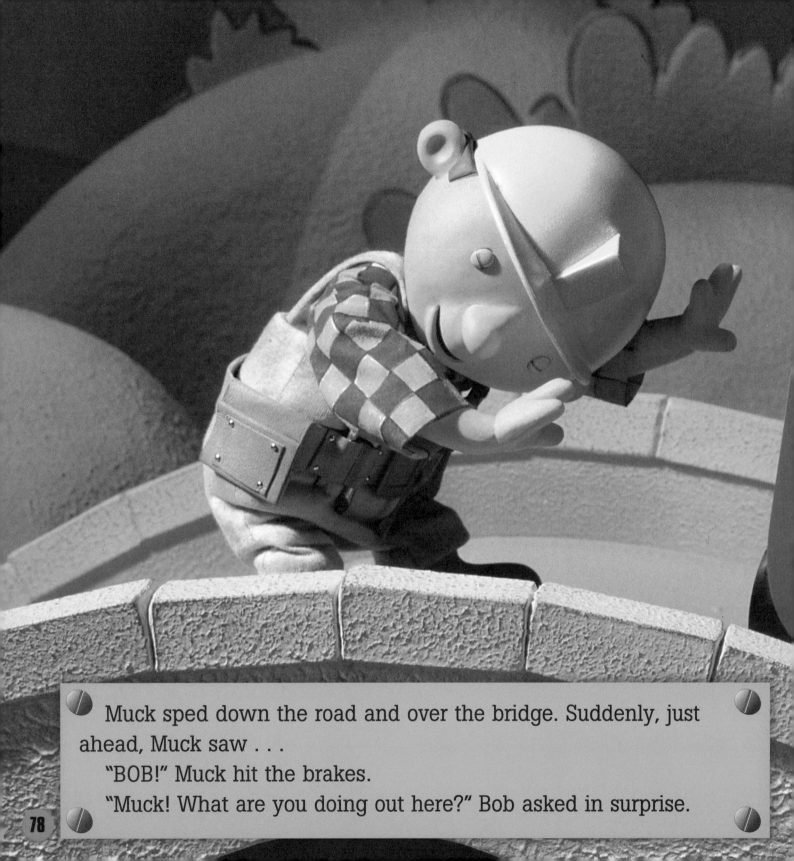

Muck sped down the road and over the bridge. Suddenly, just ahead, Muck saw . . .

"BOB!" Muck hit the brakes.

"Muck! What are you doing out here?" Bob asked in surprise.

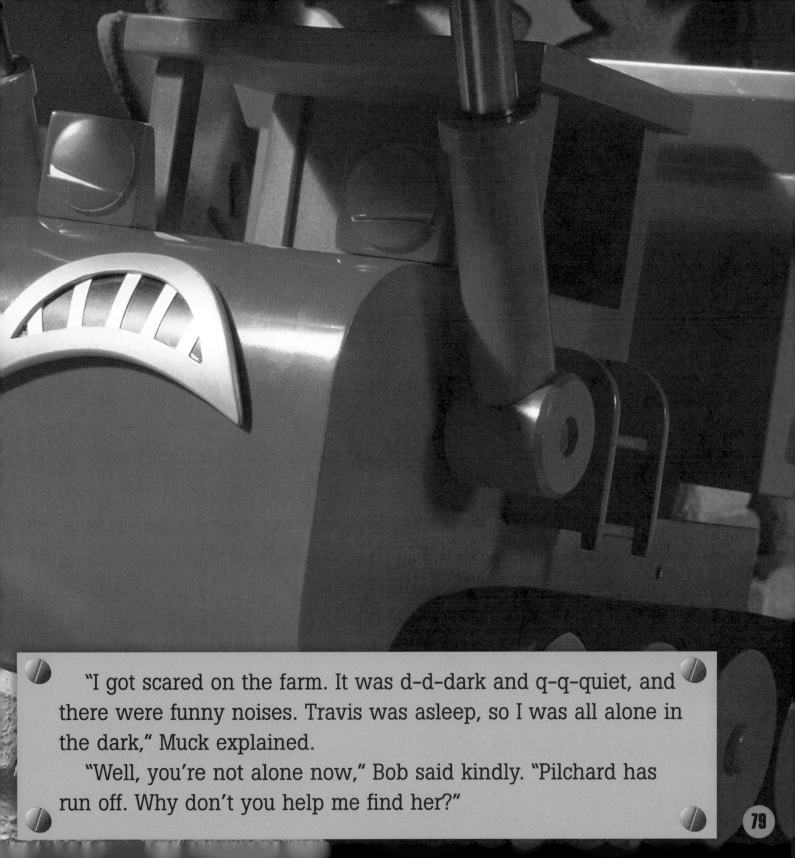

"I got scared on the farm. It was d–d–dark and q–q–quiet, and there were funny noises. Travis was asleep, so I was all alone in the dark," Muck explained.

"Well, you're not alone now," Bob said kindly. "Pilchard has run off. Why don't you help me find her?"

Nearby, Spud had lost his way in the dark. It was quiet and spooky. A bush rustled. "M-M-Muck, is that you?" Spud stammered.

"Hoot! Hoot!" said the owl from a nearby fence post.

"AHHHH!" Spud cried. "A hooting monster!" Spud jumped up and dashed off.

"MEEOOW!" screeched Pilchard, surprised.

Pilchard ran toward the road. When she spotted Bob she leaped into his arms. "Ho-ho," Bob laughed. "Where did you come from?"

"Purr, purr," said Pilchard, happy to have found her friend.

"Now we can finish the job," said Bob. "Come on, Muck, you can help."

When their work was done Bob took Muck back to Farmer Pickles's farm.

"But I won't be able to sleep in the dark," Muck said with a sigh.

"Don't worry, Muck." Bob said. "I've got a plan."

Muck settled next to the shed where Travis was sleeping.

"Good night, Muck," said Scoop and Lofty.

"Er . . . 'night, everyone," Muck said, sounding a little confused.

Then Bob pushed a button. The work lights came on, lighting up the shed as bright as day.

"Now there's no reason to be afraid of the dark!" laughed Bob.

And in no time at all Muck fell fast asleep. **"Zzzzzzz."**

Bob the Builder

Dizzy and Muck Work It Out

Bob and Wendy had just finished plastering Mrs. Broadbent's wall.

"The plaster's drying nicely," Bob said. "We should be able to paint it this afternoon."

"Oh, good," said Wendy. "I need to run over to Mrs. Potts's house. She's asked me to lay a new path in her garden."

Wendy hurried back to the building yard to get the team. Muck, Roley, and Dizzy were loaded up and ready to go.

"Can we pave it?" Wendy asked.
"YES, WE CAN!" the team shouted excitedly.

When they got there, Wendy asked Mrs. Potts where she would like the new path in her garden to go.

Mrs. Potts wasn't sure. "I want it to go near my statues. . . ."

"Which are your favorites?" asked Wendy.

"Oh, the Greek god and Cheeky Charlie!" Mrs. Potts told Wendy proudly.

"Then the new path should definitely go near those two!" replied Wendy.

"Wonderful!" Mrs. Potts cried. "Just be extra careful of Cheeky Charlie, and make sure you don't flatten my flower beds."

"Don't worry, we'll take care of everything," Wendy reassured her.

Mrs. Potts still seemed unsure, but she had to go to the store to pick up some groceries, so she left.

The team went to work.

Just then Wendy's cell phone rang. "Hi, Bob! . . . The plaster's dried? . . .
Okay, I'll get Roley to give me a lift. See you soon."

Wendy went back outside
and instructed Muck and Dizzy
to lay the paving stones on
the path while she was gone.

"You're going to leave Muck and Dizzy on their own?" Roley asked as they drove back to Mrs. Broadbent's house.

"Just for a little while," replied Wendy.

"Uh–oh," Roley said quietly. He knew what trouble Muck and Dizzy could get into together.

"Is everything all right in Mrs. Potts's garden?" Bob asked Wendy.

"Yes," replied Wendy. "I left Muck and Dizzy in charge of laying the paving stones."

Bob was surprised. "Do you think it's a good idea to leave those two alone? You know how they get into trouble sometimes."

"They'll be fine," Wendy reassured him.

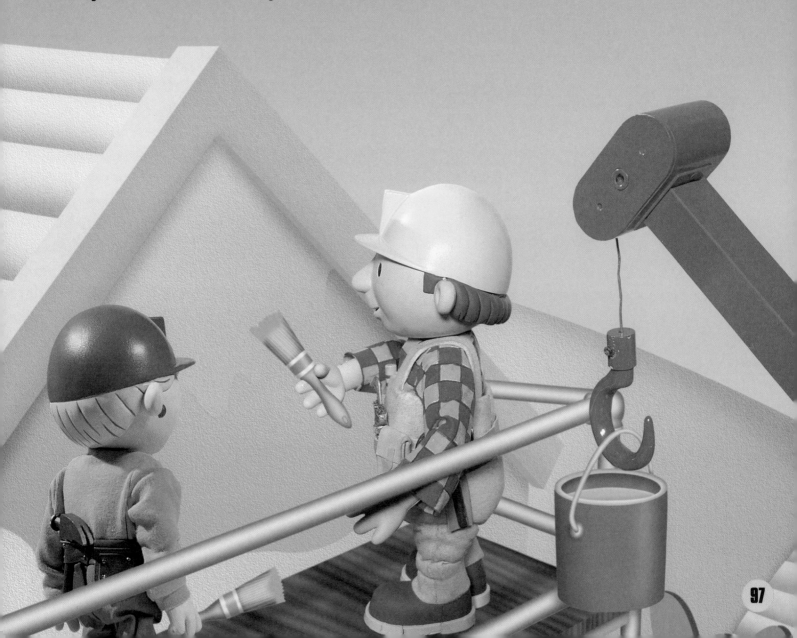

But Muck and Dizzy
weren't fine.

"Okay, let's go, Muck!"
Dizzy said in a bossy voice.

"Hey, Wendy said for us
to do this *together!*" Muck
replied, rumbling toward
Dizzy.

"Watch out for Cheeky Charlie!"
Dizzy shouted.

Muck swerved to avoid hitting
Cheeky Charlie, and the paving
stones flew into the air . . .

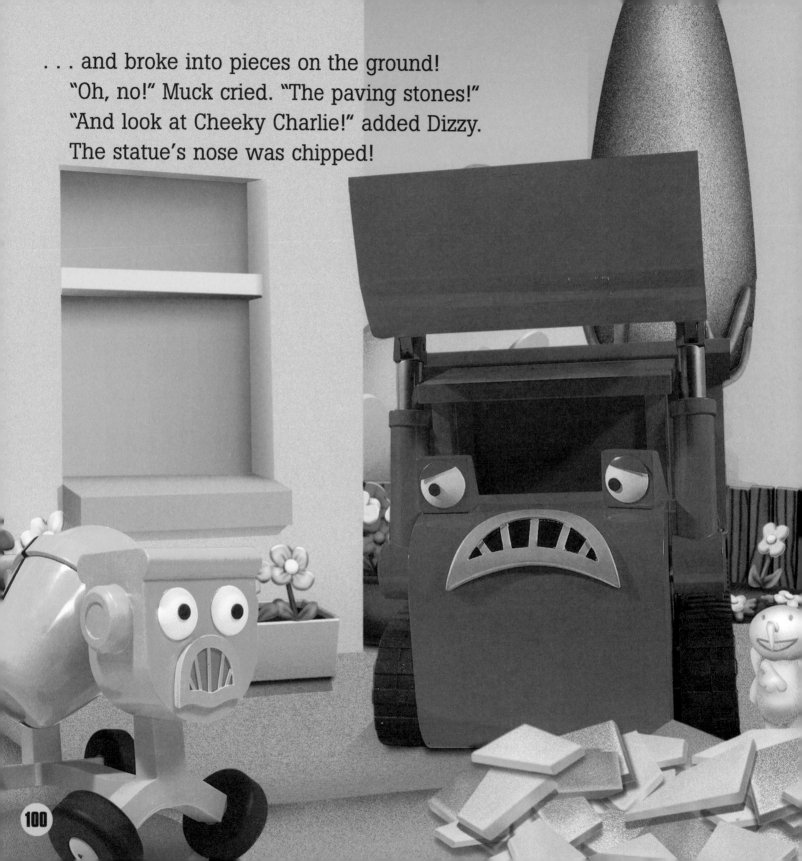

. . . and broke into pieces on the ground!
"Oh, no!" Muck cried. "The paving stones!"
"And look at Cheeky Charlie!" added Dizzy.
The statue's nose was chipped!

Back at Mrs. Broadbent's house, Bob was still worried about Muck and Dizzy.

"Maybe I'd better check to see how things are going at Mrs. Potts's garden," Wendy suggested.

"Good idea!" Bob said, relieved.

"Oh, no!" Wendy cried when she arrived. "Now what are we going to do?"
"I have an idea!" said Dizzy. "We can use the broken stones to make a path."
"Crazy paving!" Wendy exclaimed.
"You mean crazy *Dizzy*." Muck laughed.

"No, crazy paving is when you make a path out of broken paving stones," Wendy explained.
"Hee, hee, it's Dizzy's crazy paving!" Muck said.
"Yippee!" cheered Dizzy. "Let's get to work!"

Working together, Muck and Dizzy got the job done.
"Hey, it looks great!" Muck exclaimed. "You're really clever, Dizzy!"
"Thanks, Muck," replied Dizzy. "But I couldn't have done it without you!"

When Bob finished painting Mrs. Broadbent's wall, he decided to see
how Mrs. Potts's garden path was coming along.

"Hi, Bob," said Mrs. Potts, who was just coming home from the store.
"What perfect timing! Let's go see my new garden path together!"

Bob and Mrs. Potts couldn't believe their eyes.
"You've made crazy paving!" Bob exclaimed. "Good job, everyone!"
Mrs. Potts clapped her hands with excitement. "It's so pretty!"

"Whose idea was it to use those little pieces of stone?" Mrs. Potts asked.
"It was *our* idea!" Muck and Dizzy said together. Then they looked at
Wendy.

"Actually, we had an accident and we broke the paving stones," Muck confessed. "We're sorry!"

"That's okay," said Mrs. Potts. Then she looked at her new path and smiled warmly. "I think your accident made a beautiful surprise! And I always thought Cheeky Charlie's nose was too big anyway!"

"That's our team," said Wendy with a smile. "We're always coming up with *smashing* ideas!"

Bob the Builder™

Bob Saves the Porcupines

One day Spud and Travis were playing in the fields when Travis spotted something interesting.

"Hey, Spud," Travis called. "Look what I found—a family of upside-down hairbrushes!"

"They're not hairbrushes—they're porcupines!" said Spud, laughing.

Meanwhile, back at Farmer Pickles's house Bob and the team were fixing a road.

Muck was backing up noisily.

"Left a bit . . . right a bit!" yelled Bob.

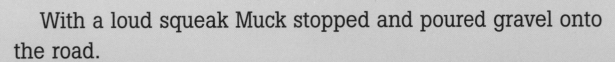

With a loud squeak Muck stopped and poured gravel onto the road.

"Great job!" shouted Bob. "Now, Scoop, I need you to spread the gravel evenly to give the road a nice new surface."

With a mighty heave Scoop pushed the pile of gravel across the road.

"Roley, it's all yours!" called Bob. "Roll the surface nice and flat!"

Roley was just about to roll over the stones when suddenly Bob spotted the porcupines.

"Roley, look out!" Bob shouted. "There are porcupines on the road!"

Roley screeched to a halt.

"Porcupines? Where?" Roley asked.
"Right under your nose!" cried Scoop.

"Now what are we going to do?" asked Bob. "We can't open this road to traffic. These porcupines won't be safe."

"How can we help the porcupines cross the road safely?" Scoop asked.

"Maybe we can build a bridge, so they can go *over* the road?" Muck suggested.

"Don't think *over!*" cried Scoop. "Think *under!*"

"That's a great idea, Scoop!" Bob exclaimed. "We'll build a tunnel, so that the porcupines can go *under* the road. Let's get to work."

"What are the porcupines going to do while we work?" asked Muck.

"Good point," said Bob. "Take them to the yard for now, Muck. And when you come back, bring some pipes with you, please."

Back at the office Wendy's phone rang.

"Bob's building yard," she answered.

"Hello, Wendy," said Bob. "I'm just calling to tell you that Muck's coming over to the yard—with a family of porcupines!"

"Okay, Bob," said Wendy.

Muck chugged along the road, scoop raised high, so that the porcupines could have a good look around.

"Hi, Muck," called Dizzy when Muck arrived back at the yard. "What are you doing back so early?"

"I'm on a porcupine rescue," Muck replied, proudly lowering them to the ground.

"Aaagh!" cried Lofty. "Mice with spikes!" He was scared.

"No, silly!" said Wendy, laughing as she came outside. "They're not mice—they're porcupines!"

Then she set a bowl of water on the ground for the porcupines to drink.

"Now, Muck, you better get going. Bob said he needed those pipes right away!"

Back at the road Bob was deciding where to put the tunnel.

"You can start digging where my tape measure ends," he told Scoop.

"How are we going to get the porcupines back here?" asked Roley.

"I spoke to Wendy," Bob replied, smiling. "She's got a plan."

"It's time for you to go home, little ones!" said Wendy to the porcupines.

"Who's going to get them there?" asked Lofty, puzzled.

"*You're* going to take them," Wendy announced.

"Me?!" said Lofty with a gulp.

Wendy smiled and carefully loaded the porcupines into a basket, which she hung from Lofty's hook.

Lofty rode slowly through town with the basket. After a little while he was so happy to be helping that he forgot to be scared of the porcupines at all.

Back at the road Lofty carefully lowered the basket of porcupines.
"I hope the porcupines like what we've done for them," said Scoop.
"Now they will always be able to cross the road safely," said Bob.
"Bye, porcupines!" shouted the machines as the porcupines scurried into the tunnel. "Good luck!"

Wendy's Big Game

One morning Bob had some news for the team. "Hello, everyone!" he said. "I've entered us in the Brightest Building Yard competition, and we have to clean up before the judges arrive."

"When are they coming?" asked Roley.

"Five o'clock," Bob replied.

"You'd better get started then," said Wendy. "Muck can help you, Bob. The rest of the machines can come with me. We've got to get the soccer field ready."

"**Can we do it?**" Wendy yelled as they roared out of the yard.

"**Yes, we can!**" cried the machines.

When Wendy and the machines got to the field, Scoop began to unload the cans of white paint. Wendy filled up the line-marking machine.

"I need to get this grass as flat as I can," said Roley. "If I leave any bumps, the ball will bounce all over the place."

Wendy marked out a goal line. Scoop unloaded the wood for the goalposts, and Roley flattened the ground. But Dizzy was bored and wanted to play soccer.

Suddenly Spud jumped out from behind a bush. "I'll play with you!" he said.

Dizzy passed the ball to Spud, who gave it a huge kick! The ball flew high into the air, then dropped slowly down.

"Oh, no!" squeaked Dizzy. "It's going to land on Wendy!"

Wendy looked up just in time and saw the ball heading straight at her. Dragging the line-marking machine, Wendy ducked sideways. The ball missed her by only a few inches!

"Where did that come from?" she asked.

"Uh, Wendy," said Scoop, "look what you've done."

Wendy gasped when she saw the wiggly line she'd made on the field. "Sorry, Wendy," said Spud. "I was just showing Dizzy a few soccer tricks." "Well, now you can get a bucket and brush and show Dizzy a few cleaning-up tricks," Wendy said.

Back at the house, Bob was busy clearing the yard. He had swept up a huge pile of garbage—and Pilchard found it! She curled up on a warm, sunny spot on top of the pile and was soon fast asleep.

Muck came roaring back into the yard with a front dumper full of plants and flowers. "Here I am, Bob!" cried Muck.

"Well done, Muck," said Bob. "Let's unload those plants. Then you can clear away that pile of garbage."

While Bob arranged his flowerpots, Muck scooped up the garbage in the back dumper.

"Me-ow!" cried Pilchard.

Bob turned around. "Oh, no! Muck, stop!" he yelled. "You've scooped up Pilchard with the garbage!"

Muck slammed on the brakes, and garbage went flying all over the yard. "Sorry, Pilchard," said Muck. "I didn't know you were up there."

Bob brought Pilchard down safely.

While Bob was hanging a flower basket, Bird settled into it.

Tweet! he chirped happily.

"Bird, I know my pots make a lovely nest, but you're squishing my flowers," said Bob.

Bird flew off, but Bob found him a few minutes later on top of another plant.

"You're squishing those flowers too, Bird," Bob said, sighing. "I don't think I'll ever have the yard clean and ready by five o'clock!"

Meanwhile, Wendy and the team were almost done with the soccer field. Lofty had lifted the goalposts into place. Roley had flattened the field perfectly. Scoop had helped Wendy build the bleachers, and Spud had even cleaned up the wiggly white line.

"Oh, Wendy," Dizzy squeaked. "Can we please play a game?"
Wendy checked her watch. "Well, we've got time. We don't have to be back at the yard until five."
"Yippee!" cried Dizzy as she raced down the field after the ball.

Wendy blew the whistle to start the game. Dizzy kicked off. And when Lofty got the ball, Dizzy jumped in and sent it up the field to Spud. Spud trapped the ball and headed it over to Wendy. Wendy dribbled the ball toward the goal—and kicked it in!

"Goal!" yelled Dizzy. "Hooray for Wendy!"

"Oh, that was fun!" said Wendy. "But we must get back to the yard. It's almost five."

Bob's yard was finished in time too. It looked very neat and clean, but Bob was covered in dirt! "I'd better clean up before the judges arrive," he told Muck.

Just then they heard a car driving up. "Oh, no," said Bob. "The judges are here early!"

Wendy and the machines came back to the yard and were surprised to see how clean and neat it looked. "Bob did a great job," said Wendy.

Suddenly Bird landed on one of the flowerpots. "Bird, get out of there before the judges arrive," Wendy said.

"It's too late," Bob said. "The judges have already come and gone."

"Really?" asked Wendy. "What did they say?"

Bob held up an award. "We won!" he exclaimed. "Our yard won first prize in the Brightest Building Yard competition!"

The machines cheered. "Whoo-hoo! Yippee!"

"Oh, Bob, that's wonderful," said Wendy. "Well done!"

"The yard looks clean, Bob," said Dizzy,
"but you're all dirty."

"Lucky for you it wasn't the Brightest
Builder competition," said Wendy, laughing.

"You're right about that, Wendy!" Bob said

Bob the Builder

Roley and the Rock Star

"Wow! It's going to be really hot today!" said Bob. It was a very sunny morning. Bob looked at the thermometer on his wall.

Bob's fish, Finn, splashed the water with his tail. "I wish I could swim around all day and keep cool like you!" said Bob, laughing.

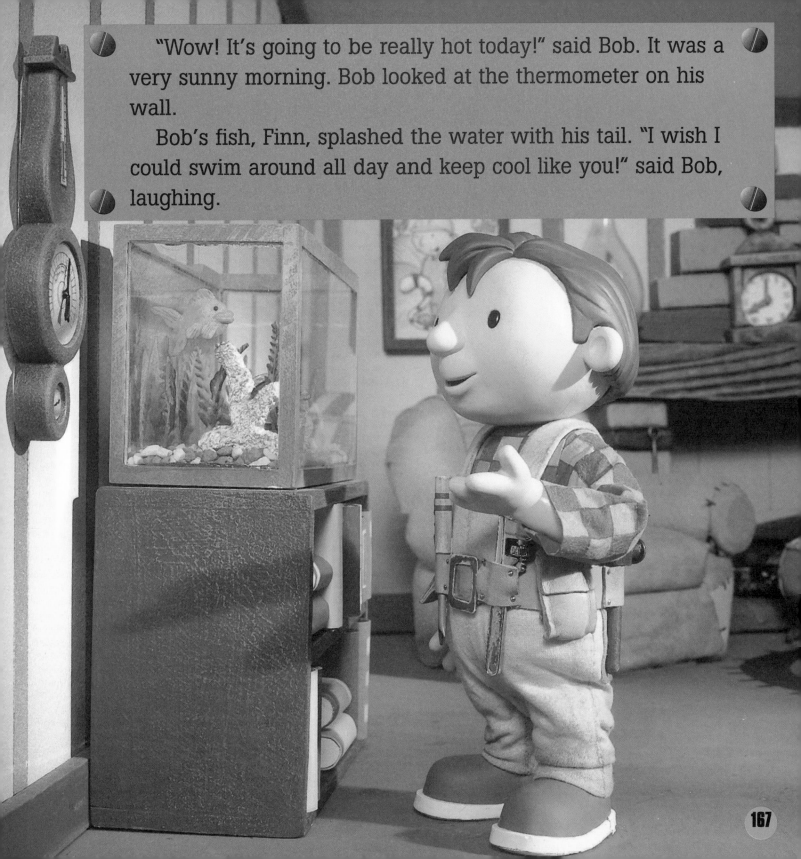

Bob went out into the yard. "Morning, everyone! We've got two big jobs to do today," he told the machines.

"I've got to make a pond in Mr. Lazenby's backyard, and Wendy's laying out a nature trail in the park."

"Wow!" Roley rumbled. "Lennie Lazenby is the lead singer of the Lazers. They're my favorite band!"

"Come on then, team. Let's go!" said Bob.

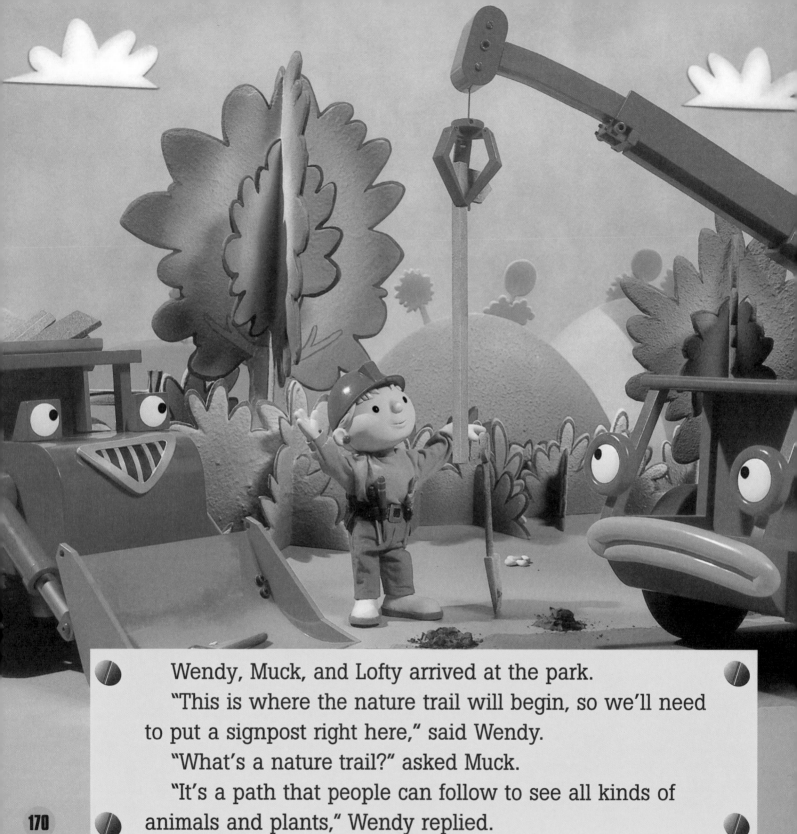

Wendy, Muck, and Lofty arrived at the park.
"This is where the nature trail will begin, so we'll need to put a signpost right here," said Wendy.
"What's a nature trail?" asked Muck.
"It's a path that people can follow to see all kinds of animals and plants," Wendy replied.

While Wendy and Muck were studying the map, a little duck suddenly popped out in front of Lofty.

"**Quack**," said the duck.

"Ooooh!" Lofty wailed.

"What's the matter, Lofty?" asked Wendy.

"A great big quacking thing just jumped out at me!" he cried.

"A duck?" asked Wendy. But the duck had hopped back into the bushes.

"I don't see any ducks. You must be dreaming, Lofty," said Muck.

Lofty kept a lookout for quacking things while Muck and Wendy built a fence.

Just then two little ducks waddled up to Muck.
"Look! Ducks!" said Muck.
"Quack! Quack!" said the ducks.

Then another duck appeared on top of Lofty!

"Lofty, you were right," said Wendy. "Hello, little duck!"

"Ooooh, Wendy! Take it away!" Lofty yelled.

"You silly goose, Lofty," said Wendy. "The ducks are more frightened of you than you are of them! Come on, team, let's take them back to the water."

Meanwhile at Lennie Lazenby's house, Bob, Dizzy, and Roley could hear loud music.

"It makes me want to dance!" said Dizzy.

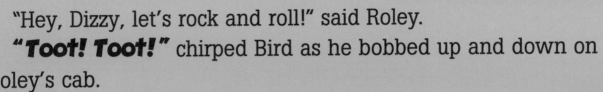

"Hey, Dizzy, let's rock and roll!" said Roley.
"Toot! Toot!" chirped Bird as he bobbed up and down on Roley's cab.

177

While Roley and Dizzy were dancing, Scoop dug a big hole
for the pond, and Bob lined it with a waterproof sheet.

"I'll need lots of cement for the fountain next to the pond,"
Bob told Dizzy.

"Cement coming up!" said Dizzy.

Lennie Lazenby came out into the yard.

"Hello, Mr. Lazenby," said Bob.

"Oh, Lennie," said Roley, rushing up. "I really dig your music!"

"Cool! Maybe we should jam sometime," said Lennie.

"Wow! That would be great," said Roley.

"Isn't he cool?" Roley said as Lennie walked away.

"Yes, but he doesn't look like the kind of person who would make jam," said Bob.

"Ha, ha, ha!" laughed Roley. "Lennie doesn't make jam. Jamming is when people get together to play music!"

"Oh, *that* kind of jam," said Bob. "Silly me!"

Back at the park, Wendy found that the duck pond had dried up.

"Poor ducks. They must have been looking for a new home!" said Muck.

"Let's see if there's room for them at the pond that Bob is building for Lennie Lazenby," said Wendy.

"Hi, Bob," said Wendy when they arrived at Lennie Lazenby's house.

"Hi, Wendy," said Bob.

"Quack! Quack!" said the ducks in Muck's scoop.

"Mr. Lazenby, the duck pond in the park has dried up," said
Wendy. "Do you think the ducks could stay in your pond?"
"Great idea! Ducks are, like, really groovy!" said Lennie.

"Aw, thanks, Lennie!" said Muck, gently sliding the
ducks into the pond.

Everyone gathered around to see if the ducks liked their
new home.

"Quack! Quack! Quack!" said the ducks as they
happily splashed around in the water.

"Hey, let's celebrate!" said Lennie. "Should I sing my new single?"

"Yes, please! That would be cool!" exclaimed Roley.

Lennie started to play his electric guitar. Bob, Wendy, and all the machines danced around the yard to Lennie's music.

"Bob the Builder, can we fix it?" sang Bob.

"Bob the Builder, yes, we can!" Wendy sang back.

Soon all the machines joined in.

"Hey, groovy singing, Roley!" said Lennie. "Maybe you could sing on my next album."

"Wow! I'd love that," said Roley.

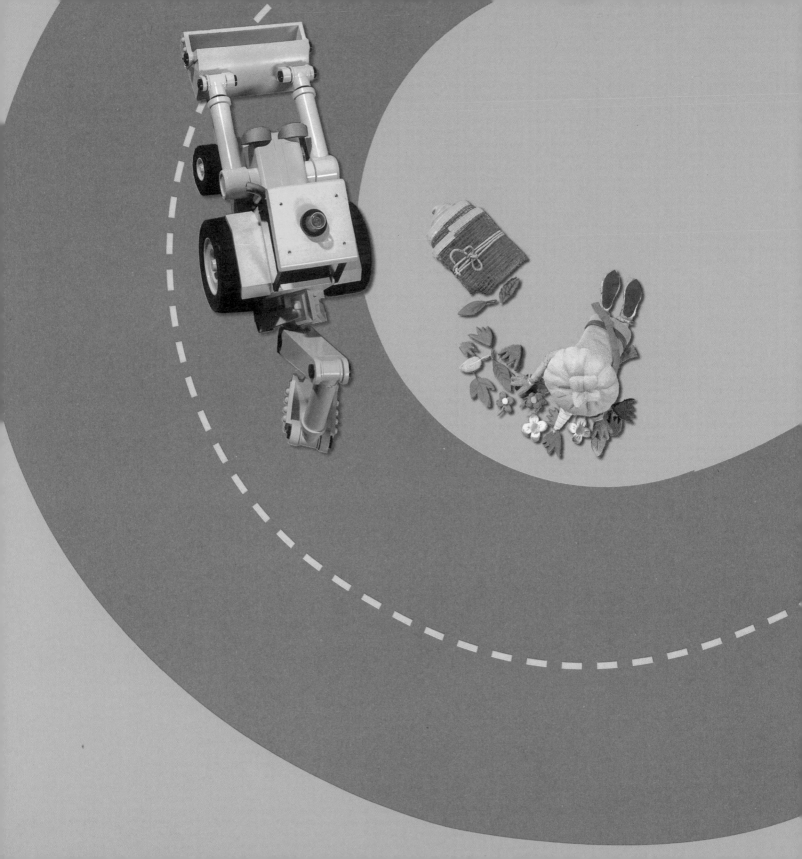